Third
Grade
stinks!

THIRD GRADE STINKS!

COLLEEN O'SHAUGHNESSY MCKENNA

illustrated by

STEPHANIE ROTH

Holiday House / New York

To my husband, JAY,
who is the most honest, loving,
and intelligent man I know
Happy Anniversary!
C. O. M.

To Leslie Fitzgerald,
my best friend in the third grade
S. R.

(with special thanks to
Groven Heights Elementary school)
S. R.

Text copyright © 2001 by Colleen O'Shaughnessy McKenna
Illustrations copyright © 2001 by Stephanie Roth
All Rights Reserved
Printed in the United States of America
First Edition
www.holidayhouse.com

Library of Congress Cataloging-in-Publication Data

McKenna, Colleen O'Shaughnessy.
Third grade stinks! / by Colleen O'Shaughnessy McKenna;
illustrated by Stephanie Roth.—1st ed.
p. cm.
Summary: Gordie loves his third grade teacher,
but sharing a locker with a girl instead of his best friend
and trouble with a school bully may ruin his best year ever.
ISBN 0-8234-1595-3
[1.   Schools—Fiction. 2.   Behavior—Fiction.] I. Roth, Stephanie, ill. II. Title.
PZ7.M1983 Th 2001
[Fic]—dc21
00-048224

chapter

"Doug, wake up." Gordie tugged his brother's leg. "Open your eyes. Come on. School starts today."

"Mmmuhmm?" Doug flipped over and yawned. Then he hid his head under the pillow. "Be quiet, Shrimp."

"I can't be late on the first day!" Gordie grabbed Doug's legs and tried to drag him off the bed.

Doug kicked his legs, sending Scratch flying into the air. The dog quickly scooted under the bed.

"Come on, Doug. Get up. I need to turn on the light to make sure I'm dressed all right," said Gordie. "Do I look like a third grader?"

Doug yawned again—a big, loud, smelly yawn. Gordie stepped back. Doug's breath smelled like the corn chips he had eaten last night.

"Can I turn on the light?"

"Only if you want me to lock you in the closet." Doug peered at the clock. "Gordie, it's four o'clock in the morning! Teachers aren't awake yet. Bus drivers aren't awake yet. Go back to bed."

"I'm not tired. My whole morning is planned. I still need to sharpen some pencils, pack lunch, and . . ."

Gordie held up his planner book. "Here's how today is supposed to go: Number one plan is to get up early for first day. Get up by 4:30 AM. Be dressed by 5:00 AM. Eat cereal, but don't eat too much in case you throw up. Finish eating at 5:20 AM. Play with Scratch ten minutes. Walk to bus stop by 6:00 AM."

Doug flopped back in the bed. "Shrimp, I promise to wake you by seven. The bus comes at seven-forty. That's plenty of time."

Gordie dropped his backpack. *Thunk.* He walked over to his bed and sat down.

Scratch whined as he crawled out from under Doug's bed, the empty bag of corn chips in his mouth. "Hi, Scratch. Today I start third grade."

"Stop worrying," grumbled Doug. "Third grade is a breeze."

"We have to learn cursive writing, Doug. Did you forget about that?"

"Cursive is a breeze. Go to sleep."

Gordie sighed. "Okay, but promise to wake me up on time."

"Okay. I promise."

Gordie took off his shoes and tried to lie down without getting wrinkled. He didn't want his teacher to think he was messy. Messy kids weren't picked to decorate bulletin boards or pass out papers.

Gordie shut his eyes. "Hey, Doug. Maybe you should wake me up before you wake yourself up."

"Very funny."

"Good night, Doug." Gordie laughed. "I mean, good morning."

Doug yawned again. "I can't believe summer is over."

Scratch hopped onto Gordie's bed. "Say good-morning to Scratch."

"Good-morning-to-Scratch." Doug cracked up. "You stinky dog."

Gordie flung his arm around the dog. "Don't hurt his feelings!"

"Too early for feelings," Doug mumbled. "At four in the morning, feelings are still asleep."

Gordie laughed. Maybe he'd be as funny as Doug when he got to fifth grade.

Gordie flipped over to his left side. His fingers closed around the smooth plastic of his new planner book.

So far Gordie had filled four of its pages.

Gordie flipped over to his right side. He hugged his planner. His heart pounded against it like a drum. The planner was filled with good plans for third grade. On page one, he had printed: GET UP EARLY FOR FIRST DAY. Even though it was dark as ink in the bedroom, Gordie knew his other plans by heart.

On page two, he had printed: MAKE SURE MISS TINGLE IS YOUR TEACHER. On page three, he had underlined: MAKE SURE I SHARE A LOCKER WITH LAMONT HAYES. Gordie yawned and whispered page four: "I plan that third grade will be the best year in my whole life."

Gordie flipped his pillow to the cool side. He yawned again. So did Scratch.

"Won't be long now, Scratch," whispered Gordie. "I'll wake you as soon as Doug wakes me. I promise."

Scratch thumped his tail, hard.

"Quiet, Shrimp, or I'll unplug the alarm."

Gordie's eyes flew open. He knew his mom would wake him up before she went downstairs. But what if she forgot today was the first day of school? What if Dad raced downstairs to read the sports section before Doug messed it up? What if everyone forgot to wake him up?

Gordie forced his eyelids open again. He had to stay awake. Nowhere in his planner had he written: SLEEP THROUGH THE FIRST DAY OF THIRD GRADE.

Gordie followed his mother downstairs. "I got the cereal bowls out for you."

Gordie tried to eat his cereal, but he was too excited to chew. When Doug came down, he had two bowls of cereal and a muffin. Then he ate a couple of cheese crackers.

"Doug, let's go to the bus stop," said Gordie.

Doug looked at the clock. "The bus won't be here for twenty minutes. What's the rush?"

"Finish your cereal, Gordie," said Mom. She handed him a glass of orange juice.

Gordie sipped his juice and picked up his spoon. Too bad he couldn't have JELL-O or ice cream for breakfast. Slippery food went down fast, even over lumps in throats.

When Dad came down, he gave Gordie half of his muffin.

"No thanks, Dad, I'm stuffed. Anyway, third graders eat lunch early."

"You need food, Shrimp," said Doug. "I don't want to have to carry you to your classroom."

"I don't need you to walk me this year."

"Are you sure? What if you get lost? What if you end up in the supply closet with buckets and brooms?"

"I won't," said Gordie. "Room nine is right next to the water fountain. It's across from the big clock in the hall."

Doug leaned closer. "What if they moved the clock, Gordie? What if they got rid of the water fountain? What if there is no room nine?" He wiggled his eyebrows.

Gordie finally laughed.

Mom handed the boys their lunches. "Doug, don't eat your lunch on the bus. Gordie, please eat *all* of your lunch."

"I will. See you later, Mom. 'Bye, Dad. I'll probably look older when I come home today."

Mom hugged Gordie. "I hope all of your plans work out."

"They will. I'm going to put my planner back in my room. I'll add more plans when I get home."

"Come on, Shrimp," said Doug. "Let's hope someone moved the school. Then we can come home and go swimming all day."

Gordie smiled. He loved summer. Swimming in the lake with Doug and his friends had been great. Sleeping out in the backyard in a tent was spooky and cool.

But summer was over. Gordie didn't mind. He had four pages of plans for the third grade, and he could hardly wait to get started.

chapter

3

When the school bus stopped at Elm and Sheradon, Gordie scooted over, making room for his best friend, Lamont. But after six kids got on the bus, the bus driver drove away.

Gordie turned around. "Hey, Doug. Do you see Lamont?"

Doug looked out the window. "Maybe he missed the bus."

Gordie slumped down. What if Lamont were sick? What if he weren't going to school today?

A big kid with glasses poked Gordie in the shoulder. "Lamont's mom is driving him. I saw their car pass the bus stop."

"Thanks," said Gordie. He should have shoved his planner into his backpack. Then he could have added: MAKE SURE LAMONT RIDES THE BUS EACH MORNING.

Gordie pressed his nose against the window. He smiled when the bus turned onto Johnston Street. The school looked the same—the flag was flying and the school buses were in line. When the driver stopped the bus, Gordie was the first one off.

"Good-bye," he shouted.

"Hey Shrimp, wait up," Doug called from a window.

"You don't have to walk me this year," Gordie shouted. "See you later."

Gordie's backpack bounced against his back as he ran. He raced up the cement stairs and followed the other kids inside.

"Good morning, children," said the principal, Mr. Fratorolli. Gordie liked Mr. Fratorolli.

Gordie walked slowly down the hall. The hall smelled like paint and the floors were as shiny as a mirror. The water fountains were still on the left, and the big clock remained on the right.

"Here's room nine," whispered Gordie. He peeked inside and saw Miss Tingle, his teacher. Gordie had waited for her since kindergarten. Everyone said she was the nicest third-grade teacher in the world.

"Hello, Miss Tingle!" said Gordie. "I'm Gordie."

"Hello, Gordie. I taught your brother two years ago."

"I know. You gave him a pencil with his name on it."

"Miss Tingle, these are for you!"

Gordie spun around. Lucy Diaz rocked back and forth on her heels, holding a big bouquet of flowers tied with a red ribbon.

"Wow!" Gordie watched as Lucy handed the flowers to Miss Tingle. Miss Tingle smiled as she smelled them. He wished he had brought Miss Tingle a present, too. He should have brought her a jelly doughnut.

"You can keep the ribbon," added Lucy. "It's silk."

"Wow!" Gordie said again. Maybe he could find some ribbon at his house. He could wrap it around the doughnut. If he couldn't find ribbon, he would color some string with a crayon.

"Tomorrow is my birthday," said Lucy. "I'll be eight."

"I'm almost eight," added Gordie.

"Almost doesn't cut it," she threw back at him.

Miss Tingle interrupted. "We'll celebrate at lunch tomorrow."

"I'll bring in treats for everyone, if that's all right with you, Miss Tingle," Lucy said.

"We'll all sing 'Happy Birthday,'" Miss Tingle said. "And thank you for my flowers."

Gordie tried not to frown. Lucy was always showing off, trying to get teachers to like her best. Last year, she'd given Mrs. Reed a fancy candle. Teachers always did like her a lot. She *was* smart. All her papers got stickers.

Too bad Gordie had left his planner at home. If he had it out now, he'd write: GET LUCY KICKED OUT OF SCHOOL.

Gordie didn't think that would happen. But could a show-off like Lucy Diaz ruin third grade?

Would page four of his planner come true? Would third grade be the best year of his life?

chapter

"Find your seats, children," said Miss Tingle. "Each desk has a name tag."

Gordie found his desk right away. He liked his spot, which was next to the windows. Miss Tingle had printed his name very neatly. It looked as if a giant typewriter had done it. Maybe Gordie should start printing more neatly in his planner.

Lucy was already at her desk, sitting up tall as if she were in church.

"Hi, Gordie!" Lamont Hayes sat down at the desk next to him. "My mom drove me this morning. We stopped at Grandma's house. She always takes my picture when school starts."

Gordie and Lamont slapped high five. "We can sit together on the bus."

"And we can sit together in room nine," said Lamont. "I hope we get to share a locker. I have so many good baseball cards. We can tape them up."

Gordie pointed to Lucy. He tried to roll his eyes like Doug always did, but they didn't roll too much.

"What's wrong with your eyes, Gordie?" asked Lamont.

Gordie blinked a couple of times. Maybe he should keep quiet about Lucy being a pain in the neck. Lamont might think he had turned mean over the summer.

Miss Tingle flashed the lights on and off. "Take a few minutes to color your name tags. New crayons are inside your desks."

Gordie opened his crayons and ran his fingers over the sharp tops. None were broken, and none had bite marks. He pulled out his black crayon and drew Scratch lying above his printed name. Then he picked up

a green crayon and drew a giant sardine. He drew a picture of Doug chasing the sardine. He picked up his pencil and drew braces on Doug's teeth. They looked so good, he drew braces on the sardine and Scratch.

"Gordie, your picture is so dumb!" said Lucy. "Dogs don't wear braces. Pickles don't, either."

"It's not a pickle," said Gordie. "It's a sardine."

"Sardines and dogs don't wear braces," said Lucy.

"*Rich* dogs wear braces," said Gordie.

Lucy laughed. "You are so funny!"

As soon as Lucy turned around, Lamont poked Gordie. "Lucy likes you, Gordie."

"Don't ever say that again!" Gordie whispered. "Let's talk about good things. Lamont, my mom packed my favorite lunch."

"A *sardine* sandwich?" Lamont laughed. "Hey, Gordie, I hope the sardines in your sandwich aren't wearing their braces!"

Gordie frowned at his picture. Even Lamont was making fun of it.

"Look at my picture," whispered Lamont. Lamont's dog was chasing a cat. Or maybe the cat was chasing the dog. It looked a lot better than Gordie's picture. Scratch looked as if he had a fence glued to his teeth.

Gordie stretched his neck to see Lucy's name tag. It had a lot of flowers on it. They looked like the flowers she had given Miss Tingle.

Gordie wanted to bring Miss Tingle some flowers, too. Nice flowers. Not the kind you found in your yard, but the kind his dad gave his mom on her birthday. The kind you could buy in a grocery store.

Gordie picked up a yellow crayon. He drew one tiny yellow flower. That would remind him to find some flowers for Miss Tingle. He'd add a special page in his planner called "Presents for Miss Tingle."

"Very clever, Gordie." Miss Tingle tapped his nameplate with her long red fingernail.

"Thanks," said Gordie. "My dog is getting his braces off soon."

"Oh, good." Miss Tingle laughed. Her teeth were white and strong. And straight.

Lucy reached out and tapped Miss Tingle on the arm. "I drew flowers. See, I have daisies, and mums, and . . ."

Gordie stared at the back of Lucy's showoffy head. He tapped Miss Tingle's other arm. "Do you like doughnuts?"

Miss Tingle patted her stomach. "I'm getting too old to eat doughnuts, Gordie."

"How about carrots?" asked Gordie. "My mom eats those when she thinks she's fat."

Miss Tingle stopped smiling.

"Ohhhh, you called Miss Tingle a fatso," Lucy crowed.

"I did not!" Gordie shouted.

Lucy just smiled.

Miss Tingle began to smile at Gordie. But it was a small smile. Very small.

"It's okay, Gordie. I know what you meant."

But Gordie wasn't sure what he meant. Why hadn't he brought his planner to school? He needed it, because right now Lucy had her own plans. She was planning on getting Gordie in big, big trouble with Miss Tingle.

chapter

Gordie's stomach started growling in the middle of a math ditto. He looked up at the clock. Eleven-ten. He wondered when third graders ate lunch.

"Finish the math ditto in the next five minutes," said Miss Tingle. "Then I'll give out locker numbers."

Gordie sat up straighter. He forgot all about being hungry. Page three of his planner was about to come true.

Lamont clapped. "Can we decorate them any way we want?"

"You can decorate the inside," said Miss Tingle. "But make sure the decorations are tasteful."

"Tasteful?" asked Lamont. "I never tried to eat a baseball card."

Miss Tingle smiled. "Lamont, you know what I mean."

Lucy got out of her seat and hurried up to Miss Tingle. "Can I tape my birthday cards to my locker?"

"Yes, Lucy. If you have a question or comment, would you please raise your hand from your desk?"

Yeah, thought Gordie. Or just climb into your desk and stay there?

Gordie finished his ditto and rechecked it twice. He always got the most stickers on math pages. He wished he had his planner right now. He'd write his new locker number down on the first page.

Miss Tingle collected the papers and then held up a notebook. "Who wants a locker?"

Everyone's hands flew up.

Miss Tingle started to read the list. Lucy wrote each number down as if she were the secretary of room 9.

"Madelyn has locker twenty-six. Lucy

will be in locker thirty-eight. Joey has locker thirty-two, Vanessa has thirty-six, and . . . Lamont will be in forty-four."

Lamont pounded his desk. "Forty-four, a double number."

Pretty soon it would be Gordie's locker number, too.

"Amber has thirty-two, and Jesse will be in forty."

Lucy stood up, waving her sheet of paper. "But Joey is already in thirty-two."

Miss Tingle nodded. "I know. Two people will share every locker."

"Gordie can share with me," said Lamont. "We share everything, even *sardine* sandwiches."

Miss Tingle looked at her list. "No, Gordie will be in locker thirty-eight."

Gordie wrote down 38. That wasn't too far from Lamont in 44.

"Miss Tingle!" Lucy ran up to the front of the room. "Gordie can't be in thirty-eight. I'm in thirty-eight and . . . and . . ."

Miss Tingle lowered her paper. "And what, Lucy?"

"And I'm allergic to him!"

Lots of kids laughed. Gordie stared at his shoes. Too bad page three of his planner hadn't come true. Why didn't Lucy move to Ohio? Or even Alaska! Gordie looked up. Miss Tingle wasn't laughing. She was frowning at Lucy.

Lucy's face was red. "Can't I share with a girl? Boys are so messy and stinky and . . ."

Miss Tingle held up her hand. "You will share with Gordie Barr." She began reading her list again.

Lucy walked slowly back to her seat. Two girls reached out and patted her arm as if she had just found out her cat had died.

"I wanted to share a locker with you," Lamont said. "I've got some cool baseball cards from my cousin. I thought we could tape them to the inside."

Gordie drew in a deep breath. "I wanted to share with you, too. It was page three of my planner."

Lamont shook his head. "You can't plan anything in third grade. The teacher gets to make up all the rules."

"Can I trade?" Jesse asked Miss Tingle. "I ride the bus with Joey, and . . ."

Soon lots of kids were waving their hands. Everyone wanted to trade.

Miss Tingle rubbed her head as if room 9 were giving her a huge headache. Then she walked over and flashed the lights on and off. Twice!

"Everyone will stay in the locker I gave them. If you don't want to act like good third graders, then you can march down the hall and use the cubbies outside room three."

Room 9 got quiet. Nobody said a word.

Room 3 was second grade.

chapter

No one mentioned locker sharing until they were down in the cafeteria. Then everyone started talking about it.

"Lucy," called Lamont. "If you're really allergic to Gordie, why don't you have a rash?"

Lucy twisted in her seat and started to whisper to Vanessa. Both girls turned around and gave Gordie and Lamont evil-queen looks.

Lamont picked up his milk carton and tried to hide behind it. "Oh, I'm so scared of you two."

Lucy threw a pretzel. It hit Lamont on the head. Gordie cracked up. Lucy had a pretty good arm. Another pretzel hit Gordie on the nose.

Gordie's hand closed around a carrot. He was about to throw it when he remembered he had accidentally called Miss Tingle fat. It was all Lucy's fault. He had to get her out of his locker, and he had to do it fast.

"Lucy acts like a boss all the time," said Gordie. "I bet she'll use both hooks in the locker. I'll have to wad my jacket up on the shelf."

"Yeah," said Lamont. "I bet she brings in a zillion pictures of flowers and kittens."

Gordie pushed away his lunch. "What if she sprays the locker with perfume?"

He drummed his fingers on the table. There had to be a way to get Lucy out of locker 38.

"Are you going to eat your sandwich?" asked Lamont.

Gordie unwrapped his sandwich. He lifted the bread and saw five tiny sardines lying in a row. They looked like they were sleeping on a tiny white raft of bread.

"Your mom is so cool," said Lamont. "My mom would *never* make me a sardine sandwich."

Gordie bent to sniff his sandwich. "Don't you just love sardine stink?"

Lamont grinned. "Sardine stink stinks just fine."

Gordie handed half to Lamont. After one giant bite, Gordie grabbed the sandwich back.

"Hey," cried Lamont.

"Sorry, Lamont," said Gordie. "These sardines could be a secret weapon."

He looked down at his sandwich. Then he picked up the longest sardine and wrapped it in his napkin.

"What are you doing?"

Gordie peeked up and down the table. He lowered his voice. "Operation Exit."

"What are you talking about?"

"I'm going to keep this in my locker all afternoon." He slid the sardine into his pocket.

Lamont made a face. "Your whole locker is going to stink."

"That's my plan. Let's go outside. I'll put the sardine in the sun," Gordie said.

"Yuck."

"Come on. My sardine wants to get a tan."

Once they were outside, Gordie and Lamont watched Lumpy Labriola chase some fourth graders away from the slide. Then Lumpy ran down the slide, yelling and waving his arms.

"That kid is crazy," muttered Lamont. "And big."

"Yeah." Gordie added, "I'm glad I don't have to share a locker with him. He's not afraid of anything. Not even the playground monitors."

Lamont elbowed Gordie. "Come on. Let's hide the sardine before Lumpy makes sardines of us."

Gordie looked around and pointed to some rocks near the sidewalk. He walked over and put the sardine on a flat one and covered it with a leaf. "It's so hot today, Mr. Sardine should be pretty stinky, pretty fast. Operation Exit!"

"There you go again," Lamont said.

"My new plan is to get Lucy out of locker thirty-eight. She'll exit. Get it? Lucy Diaz is leaving the building."

"The sardine is going to tell her to do that?"

"Sort of," said Gordie. "The sardine is going to stink her out."

"That little sardine is no match for Lucy," hissed Lamont. "Did you see her peg us with those pretzels? Man, that girl has an arm. She'll pick up that sardine by the tail and whammo! Splat!"

"She won't know it's in the locker," Gordie said. "She'll just wonder why she smells like Charlie the tuna. She'll just wonder why ten dozen cats keep following her home from the bus stop."

"Now I get it," said Lamont.

"Maybe she'll think the locker is haunted," said Gordie. "By dead fish."

"Maybe she'll have so many nightmares, her mom will send her to a special school. One with padded walls."

Gordie laughed. "Just so she gets out of my locker."

Lamont smiled. "So it can be *our* locker."

Gordie and Lamont high-fived each other and raced toward the kickball game.

chapter

As soon as Gordie heard the recess bell, he raced over to the flat rock.

"I can hardly wait to smell our secret weapon, Lamont. I bet it smells worse than a ten-pound skunk."

The rock was there. Two leaves were there. But no sardine.

"Hey, where did it go?" Gordie raked his fingers through the grass. He found a candy wrapper, but no sardine.

"Maybe a squirrel ate it," said Lamont. "I bet they get tired of acorns."

The playground lady blew her whistle and waved for Gordie and Lamont to line up.

"Be right there, Mrs. Wozneack," called Gordie. He looked again. "Now what am I going to do?"

"Don't you have plans for when your plans don't work?" Lamont pulled on Gordie's arm. "Come on. I don't want Miss Tingle to get mad."

The two boys caught up with their class. Miss Tingle and twenty-four kids marched up the cement stairs and through the doors.

As they filed past the office, everyone looked into the glass window. A girl who looked like a fifth grader was crying. The secretary was trying to wipe something off the girl's skirt.

"Stop crying, Charlene. It's not so bad," said the secretary.

"It is, too. I sat on a fish. A fish! The boys are calling me Charlene-of-the-sea." Charlene cried harder. "My mom just bought me this skirt."

"It will come right out. Don't you worry," the secretary said.

Gordie tapped Lamont on the arm. "I hope the sardine doesn't have our finger-prints on it!"

"What was a sardine doing on the play-ground?" asked Lucy.

"Maybe he got on the wrong bus," called out Bertie Meckly.

"Now what are you going to do?" whispered Lamont.

"I'll have to find another surprise for Lucy," Gordie whispered back. "We might get in trouble if we bring more sardines to school."

"Tomorrow is gym day, children," reminded Miss Tingle. "Be sure to remember to bring your sneakers."

Gordie walked past his locker. He would remember his sneakers. But he also needed to remember he only had twenty-four hours to plan a stinky way to get Lucy Diaz out of locker 38.

chapter

Gordie ran all the way home from the bus stop. He kissed his mom and headed for the stairs.

"Hey, where are you going?" called his mother. "Tell me all about third grade. I made a snack for you and Doug."

"Doug will be here in a second. I'll be right down to tell you everything."

Gordie took the stairs two at a time. He would tell his mom about Miss Tingle. He'd tell her all about Lamont. But he couldn't tell her about Lucy or his new plan to stink a girl out of locker 38.

Gordie closed his bedroom door and hurried over to his bed. He slid his hand under his pillow. Nothing was there.

"Mom!" Gordie yelled down the stairs. "My planner is gone."

"Stop yelling," Mom said. She stood at the bottom of the stairs. "I put it on your bookshelf. Scratch was carrying it around in his mouth all day."

"Oh, great!" Gordie raced back into his room. He pulled his planner from the shelf. Bite marks were everywhere. "Bad dog!"

Scratch moaned from under the bed. Gordie got down on all fours and lifted the bedspread. Scratch closed his eyes.

"Don't try to hide from me," mumbled Gordie. "Why did you wreck my book? How am I supposed to get through the third grade without my plans?"

Scratch thumped his tail.

"Come here, boy," said Gordie. He patted the rug, and Scratch wiggled out on his belly.

"Maybe you knew my day was not following my plans. Is that why you had it in your mouth? Did you want to bring it to school to show Miss Tingle?"

Scratch rolled over onto his back. Gordie rubbed the dog's hairy tummy. With his other hand, Gordie opened his planner. So far, he had gotten up early, and he had Miss Tingle as a teacher. But he didn't get to share a locker with Lamont, and Lucy was still in room 9. Could page 4 come true?

"Things aren't too bad," admitted Gordie. "Third grade is still okay. I just have to get Lucy out of and Lamont into my locker."

The door opened. Doug stood there with a cupcake in his hand. "Can I eat your cupcake?"

Gordie nodded. "Okay."

"Thanks, Shrimp. Why don't you get changed, and we can toss the football around later? I'll show you how so you won't embarrass me on the playground."

Gordie stood up. "First let me stick my new sneakers into my backpack. I don't want to forget them."

"Good work, Gordie," said his mom from the doorway. "Doug, eat in the kitchen."

Doug shoved the whole cupcake into his mouth. Mom shook her head and walked away.

Gordie opened the closet door and looked inside. He saw his dress shoes, his boots, and his brand-new sneakers. The sneakers smelled like a shoe store.

Gordie put the sneakers on his bed. He went back to the closet. He picked up one of his boots. It smelled terrible, like sour milk.

"Boy, these stink," said Gordie. "I wore them in the lake!"

"Let me smell," said Doug. He took a deep breath. "You better bury those in the yard."

Gordie laughed. "Are they the stinkiest shoes in the whole world?"

"No. My old sneakers are even worse. Mom threw them out yesterday. I bet the garbage men won't let them in their truck."

Gordie put his sneakers into his backpack. Suddenly he sat up straight.

"Doug, what did Mom do with your old sneakers?"

"She took them outside. She said the closet would end up smelling like a dump."

"Wow! I'd like to smell them!"

"You're a weird kid," said Doug. "Check the trash can."

Gordie raced past Doug and went downstairs. His mother was talking on the phone. Good. She wouldn't want to see Gordie digging through the trash cans. He couldn't tell her of his plan to stink Lucy out of locker 38.

Gordie walked back down the stairs. First he had to find the sneakers. Next he had to hide them until school tomorrow.

Three trash cans were lined up by the garage.

Which can has the sneakers? wondered Gordie. He lifted the lid of the first can and smelled. It just smelled like regular garbage.

Gordie opened the second lid. It was filled with junk from the garage. Dad and Doug had filled up the whole can on Saturday.

Gordie worked his way through the third can. "Where are those sneakers?" muttered Gordie. He stared down at coffee grounds and eggshells. He pushed aside a lawn bag filled with weeds from the yard. He lifted a smaller bag and peered inside the can.

"Yippee!" cried Gordie. Doug's sneakers were on the bottom. Gordie put all the garbage back carefully. He picked up Doug's shoes by the laces. He dangled them in front of his nose and took a deep breath. They smelled terrible.

"Phew!" Gordie started to cough. Doug's shoes smelled worse than the dump. They smelled just like a dead fish Gordie had found on the beach.

"These will do the trick," said Gordie. He held the sneakers out in front of him.

Gordie tiptoed to the bushes. He would hide the sneakers there overnight. In the morning, he'd stuff them into his backpack. As soon as he got to school, he would hide them in locker 38.

Lucy will want a new locker right away,

thought Gordie. He dropped the sneakers behind a bush. All he had to do now was run back inside and write his new plan down.

But when he looked up, he saw his mom frowning at him.

chapter

"Gordie Barr!" cried his mother. "What are you doing with Doug's stinky sneakers?"

Gordie's heart stuck in his throat. He looked at the bush. Doug's sneakers were sticking out.

"I need Doug's shoes for school," said Gordie.

"Sweetie, Dad and I bought you brand-new sneakers."

"I know," said Gordie. "But Doug's shoes smell like dead fish. Those are really great shoes."

Mom walked down the steps and picked up Doug's sneakers. She carried them back to the trash, holding them as far away as

possible. "These are *not* great shoes. These are trash shoes. Much too smelly for school."

"Don't give them away." Gordie ran over to the trash cans. "Let me have them. I love smelly stuff."

Mom opened a trash bag. She dropped the shoes inside. "Don't be silly. Miss Tingle would not like you to stink up the third grade."

She pointed to the back door. "Now let's go back inside and wash our hands."

Gordie followed her. He washed his hands two times.

"Now, tell me all about your day, Gordie. Did things go as planned?"

Gordie shook his head. And now his plan for tomorrow was outside in the trash can. He would have to sneak out and hide the sneakers all over again.

"Do you like third grade?" asked Mom.

"Yes," said Gordie. "I love it. All except for one thing."

"What is the one thing you don't like?"

Gordie tapped his fingers on the table. What if his mom got mad at him?

"It's nothing," said Gordie.

Mom reached out and patted his hand. "I wish you would tell me. Maybe I could help."

"Do you have some stinky shoes I could borrow?" asked Gordie.

"What on earth are you talking about?"

Gordie slumped in his chair.

"Gordie, sweetie. I'm your mom. You can tell me about any problem. What's wrong?"

Gordie wished he could run upstairs and plan a new plan in his book. The only problem was, he didn't have the right plan to get rid of Lucy.

chapter

Gordie knew his mom would sit at the table with him until he told her what was wrong. Luckily the phone rang, and she went to answer it. Gordie stayed at the table, trying to think of a new plan.

"Hey, Gordie!"

Lamont pressed his face against the screen door. "Hi. Want to go get a pack of baseball cards?" Gordie and he collected baseball cards. They each had two shoe boxes filled with them. Doug had given them some of his old ones, because he only kept the good cards.

Gordie opened the door. "I have to ask my mom first. She might be mad at me."

Lamont looked at the plate of cupcakes. "Those sure look good."

Gordie handed him one.

"Thanks." Lamont took a big bite. "Why is your mom mad? Did you tell her about the squashed sardine?"

"No. But I got Doug's old sneakers from the trash and hid them in the bushes. I wanted to take them to school, for Operation Exit. But my mom saw me."

"Too bad," said Lamont. "I bet his sneakers smelled real bad."

Gordie nodded. "Yeah. They were the best stinky shoes I ever smelled."

Five minutes later, Mom walked into the kitchen. "Hello, Lamont. How do you like third grade?"

"I love it. Gordie and I sit right beside each other. And our lockers are only six doors apart." Lamont looked at the cupcakes again. "You sure make nice-looking cupcakes, Mrs. Barr. They must taste good."

Mom picked up the plate. "Please try one."

Lamont took the biggest one on the plate. "Thank you."

"You're welcome." She set the plate down and looked at Gordie. "So tell me why you need to bring in Doug's shoes?"

"I know why," said Lamont. He licked his thumb.

Gordie didn't know what Lamont was going to say. If he said Gordie wanted to stink Lucy out of locker 38, there would be trouble.

"I'd like to know," said Mom.

Gordie closed his eyes.

"Gordie wanted to bring lots of sneakers to school," said Lamont. Cupcake crumbs were flying out of his mouth.

Mom handed Lamont a napkin. "He only has two feet."

"I know," said Lamont. "But Gordie wanted to bring in extra. He can keep them in his locker. So if somebody forgets their shoes, Gordie can loan them."

Gordie opened his eyes. Lamont's answer was pretty good and didn't tell a

big lie. Gordie *did* want to keep the stinky shoes in his locker.

"Well, those shoes are back in the trash," said Mom. "They are too stinky for third grade."

Gordie looked at Lamont. There was no way his mom would let those shoes leave the trash can. His mom hated things that stunk. She was afraid of skunks. She *hated* a type of cheese Grandad sold at his store.

Gordie's head popped up. Cheese! There was one that smelled so bad only a few people bought it each week.

"Mom, can Lamont and I walk to the store? I want to talk to Grandad."

Mom smiled. "How nice. Grandad would love that. Wait a minute—I'll wrap up two cupcakes for him."

"Great!" said Gordie.

"Does your grandad sell baseball cards?" asked Lamont.

"No, just meats and cheese. *Lots* of cheese." Gordie tried to wink at Lamont. He wanted to let him know he had a plan.

"What's wrong with your eye?" asked Lamont.

"Nothing."

"Be careful, boys," said Mom. "Remember, go straight to the store and back. Go the back way. Don't cross the road with the traffic light."

"We'll be careful." Gordie and Doug walked to Grandad's store a lot. "Mom, what's the worst-smelling cheese in the world? The one you hate?"

Mom laughed. "*Limburger.* That cheese stinks!"

"Worse than old sneakers from the trash?" asked Lamont.

"Ten times worse!" said Mom.

Gordie knew what he had to do now. As soon as he got to Grandad's store, he'd place his order. "Stinky cheese, please."

chapter

Gordie and Lamont were almost at Grandad's store when they saw Lucy.

"Quick, duck down!" Gordie pulled Lamont's arm. They both peered through a hedge.

"What is she doing here?" asked Lamont.

"I don't know," said Gordie. "She lives near school."

"Yeah. She lives in that new apartment building."

Gordie and Lamont watched as Lucy walked down the sidewalk carrying a brown bag. She was walking a large golden dog on a leash.

"Wow! Look at that dog!" whispered Lamont. "He's twice the size of mine."

That was exactly the kind of dog Gordie wanted to get to play with Scratch.

"Okay, the coast is clear." Lamont stood up and looked around. "We better run the rest of the way."

"Yeah. She might come back," said Gordie. He hopped over the hedge and ran as fast as he could. Lamont called after him, but Gordie ran faster. He wasn't Gordie anymore; he was the fastest and the best golden retriever in the world.

Gordie was so tired when he got to the store, he had to sit down. Lamont ran up and sat down beside him.

"Beat you," said Gordie.

"You got a head start," puffed Lamont. "Think your grandad will give us a free soda?"

Gordie stood up. "Sure."

Gordie opened the door. Grandad was behind the counter, piling up a little mountain of ham on the scale.

"Hello, Gordie!" sang out Grandad. "Good afternoon, Lamont."

"Hi, Grandad!" said Gordie. Because Grandad was with a customer, Gordie stood up straight and tried to smooth back his sticking-up hair.

"Hi, Mr. DeLuca," said Lamont. Lamont looked at the tiny cooler in the corner of the store. It had cans of soda, bottles of apple juice, and lots of milk.

"Get yourself a cold drink," said Grandad. "You two look mighty hot."

"We ran all the way," said Gordie.

Lamont and Gordie sat on the low window ledge, sipping their drinks and watching Grandad.

"Anything else?" he asked his customer.

"A quarter pound of my favorite cheese." The lady laughed. "I bet I'm the only one who loves this cheese so much."

Grandad grinned. "Two other customers do, Mrs. Loomis. A man from Jackson Street and a sweet lady like yourself who buys a quarter pound a week."

The bell on the door jingled as the lady left.

"Okay, come here and give me a hug!"

Grandad came from behind the counter and held out his arms.

Gordie put down his apple juice and hugged Grandad tightly.

Then Grandad went over and held out his hand to Lamont. "So, are you too big to hug me now, Mr. Third Grader?"

Lamont held out his hand, and Grandad pulled him up. He gave him a bear hug and set him down. Lamont and Gordie laughed.

"So, tell me about your day," said Grandad.

"Gordie and I sit by each other. We also have real lockers," said Lamont.

"Very good," said Grandad. "Is your teacher nice?"

"Yes," said Gordie. "We have Miss Tingle. She's the nicest teacher."

"This is wonderful," said Grandad. "So, I guess everything is perfect in the third grade."

"Almost perfect," said Gordie. "There's just one more thing I need."

"What's that?" asked Grandad. "A new backpack?"

Gordie shook his head. "No, Grandad. What I need is right here."

Gordie tapped his finger against the glass case. He was pointing to the Limburger cheese.

chapter

"Third graders need to bring in Limburger cheese?" Grandad rubbed his forehead. "When I was your age, all I needed was a pencil and some paper."

"I have pencils and paper, Grandad," Gordie said.

Lamont laughed. "We don't need it for homework. Gordie needs it for a special reason."

"Your mother doesn't like this cheese," said Grandad. "She doesn't want it in her refrigerator."

"That's why I'm taking it to school. She won't have to smell it. She won't have to even *touch* it!"

Grandad started to laugh. "Okay, so my

grandson wants to bring a Limburger sandwich for lunch. Just like I did when I was your age. This is wonderful. All right, I will get you some cheese."

"Not a sandwich . . .," Gordie started to say.

"Sandwiches are good," said Grandad. He reached into the meat cooler and pulled out the cheese. "But cheese and crackers are also good."

Gordie watched as Grandad sliced off a small piece. He wrapped it in white paper. "I only gave you a little chunk. Your mom won't want it to stay in her house long. If you want more, come back and see me tomorrow."

Gordie took the package. It was the size of a plum. The cheese was small enough to hide in his backpack.

"Thanks, Grandad." Gordie looked down at the cheese. He sniffed it. It didn't smell so stinky right now. He'd have to unwrap it as soon as he got to school. He wanted the stink to hop right out of the locker at Lucy.

The bell jingled as the two boys walked out of the store. Lamont checked his watch.

"Three-forty-five, Gordie. I better go home."

"Okay, see you tomorrow. Do you want to keep the cheese for me?"

Lamont's eyes got big. "I can't. My dog would sniff it out and eat it. You know him."

"You're right. I'll have to hide it at my house." Gordie stuck the package deep in his pocket. The paper jabbed his leg. He pulled it out and put it in his shirt pocket. The paper jabbed his heart.

"What's wrong with you, Gordie?" asked Lamont.

Gordie shook his head. "I guess I'm worried about my plan to stink Lucy out. It's too mean to write in my planner."

"She won't care."

"Yeah. She really wants to have a locker with a girl."

Lamont nodded. "Yeah. Then they can leave all their stuffed animals in there."

"Once I get rid of Lucy, I'll bring in my baseball cards. I'll tape them on the inside of the locker door."

"Me too." Lamont reached into his pocket and pulled out a stack of cards. He took the rubber band off. He must have had twenty. "Here, you can have this one," said Lamont. "I have three of him."

Gordie looked at the card. "Fastball Martinez." He had never heard of the player.

At the corner of Elm and Sheradon, Lamont turned right.

Gordie kept walking on Elm. He took the cheese out of his pocket and held it. Carrying his stinky cheese and baseball card, he passed six more houses.

By the time he got to his house, he was tired. Third grade was a lot harder than second grade. Maybe getting a locker with Lamont wasn't such a big deal. Maybe his whole life would be easier if Miss Tingle took the lockers back. Maybe he should forget his planner and go straight back to second grade.

chapter

Gordie walked up the driveway. He peeked in the kitchen window. Good, his mom wasn't there. He hurried in and stuck the Limburger cheese in the back of the refrigerator. It fit perfectly behind a large jar of grape jelly.

"Gordie, how was your trip to the store?" Mom walked past him and got a pan from the pantry. "I was just about to start dinner. How does spaghetti sound?"

Gordie looked at the refrigerator. Did his mom need anything in the refrigerator to make spaghetti?

"Or else we could just have cereal for dinner," Gordie said.

Mom laughed. *"Cereal?"*

Suddenly Gordie remembered you needed milk for cereal. The refrigerator!

"I mean, I *don't* want cereal," sputtered Gordie. "Maybe we shouldn't even have cereal in the morning. We can eat bread. Without jam."

Mom laughed. "Please set the table, honey."

Gordie got out the silverware. Should he mention the Limburger cheese to his mom? What would happen if she found it?

"Gordie, is there something wrong?"

Gordie turned. His mother was staring at him. He blinked and sat down. He had a headache. Being sneaky was hard work.

"Mom," said Gordie. "If I tell you something, try real hard not to get mad, okay?"

Mom sat down next to Gordie. "You can tell me anything."

"Well, when I was at Grandad's store . . ." Gordie stopped. He swallowed. "I got some stinky cheese. The kind you hate."

Mom looked surprised. "You got Limburger cheese?"

"It won't stay in the refrigerator long," promised Gordie. "I'm going to take it to school tomorrow. I won't even bring it home."

"I'll make you a sandwich with the cheese," said Mom. "I'll plug my nose while I make it."

"You don't have to make me a sandwich," said Gordie. "I'll just bring it in all wrapped up. Then you'll never see it again."

"You can't eat it plain, Gordie. It would be too strong. How about some crackers?"

"No, that's okay. Plain is fine."

Doug walked in, tossing his football in the air. "Hey, Shrimp. Time to toss the football with me?"

Mom stood up. "That's a great idea. Go play. I'll call you when dinner is ready."

"Well, okay," said Gordie. "But, Mom, don't touch the cheese. The stink is really bad. It might fill up the whole house. Dad will want us all to sleep in a motel."

"You are so weird," said Doug. "Come on. We'll be in the backyard, Mom."

"Have fun," his mom said. "Don't worry, Gordie. I won't even *look* at your cheese."

Gordie smiled. But his smile slipped off his face quickly. His mom wouldn't be joking if she knew what he was going to do with the cheese.

When they were outside, Gordie poked his brother on the arm. "Doug, do you like girls?"

Doug made a face. "Some girls."

"Would you like to share a locker with a girl?"

Doug laughed. "No. There wouldn't be room for any of my junk. Girls bring in brushes and lip gloss."

"I don't want to share a locker with Lucy," said Gordie. "But Miss Tingle put us together."

"Too bad," said Doug. "Just ask Miss Tingle to switch you."

"She said no."

Doug tossed the football up in the air. "Well, it's not that bad. It's not like you have to take her to a dance."

"What?" Gordie's heart flip-flopped. He didn't *ever* want to dance with Lucy. Sharing a locker with her was bad enough.

"Run out for a pass, Gordie," yelled Doug.

Gordie started running. He ran right out of the yard, into the kitchen, and upstairs to his bedroom.

He flipped open his planner and scribbled as fast as he could.

NO DANCING ALLOWED IN THE THIRD GRADE.

chapter

It was raining the next morning. Doug and Gordie raced down the sidewalk to the bus stop. Their mother had tried to drive them to the bus.

But Gordie was afraid his cheese might smell up the car. He'd stuffed it into his book bag. So far it didn't stink. Gordie hoped the bus driver wouldn't ask him to get it off the bus. But he hoped Lucy would want to get it out of locker 38.

Gordie saved a seat for Lamont on the bus. "I have the secret weapon."

"The cheese?"

"As soon as we get to school, the cheese goes to work."

When they got to school, each boy walked slowly. They didn't want to get in trouble for running. What if Mr. Fratorolli stopped them? What if he said, "Stop boys! Let me see what's in your back-packs!"

Gordie stood beside locker 38. He opened the locker. There was a pink sweater hanging from the hook. Lucy had been the first one to use the locker. She had to be the first to do everything.

"Look at her cool sneakers," said Lamont.

Lucy's white and green shoes were on the floor of the locker.

"She's taking up all the room," said Gordie. He opened his backpack and put his shoes in. They fit. He pulled off his blue jacket and hung it on a hook. It fit, too.

"I guess there's room for my stuff," said Gordie.

"Yeah. But look at this," said Lamont. He pointed to a picture of a yellow dog. Lucy had taped it to the locker door. "You need room to tape up your baseball cards."

Gordie looked at the picture. That was the dog he had seen Lucy walking. She sure was lucky to have that dog.

"Where are you going to put the cheese?" asked Lamont. "How about sticking it in her sneakers?"

Gordie smiled. Then he frowned. "Mr. Weber would be mad if Lucy stunk up his gym."

"Yeah. How about sticking it inside her sweater?"

Gordie looked at Lucy's pink sweater. *"The Pink Stink!"*

"Go on!" said Lamont.

Gordie reached in and took out the cheese. He opened the white paper. He wanted the stink to get out faster.

Gordie reached up and put the cheese on the top shelf.

"Why don't you rip it into two pieces?" said Lamont. "Stereo stink."

"Then the stinky cheese would make my hands stinky," said Gordie. "Miss Tingle would be mad."

"Hey, what are you two doing in my locker?"

Gordie and Lamont spun around. Lucy frowned at them.

"Nothing. Besides, it's *my* locker, too." Gordie closed the locker and marched past Lucy.

"Well, just don't touch my stuff," called Lucy. "My sweater is brand-new. I got it this morning for my birthday."

Gordie kept on walking.

"Aren't you going to wish me a happy birthday?" asked Lucy.

"Okay, happy birthday, Lucy," Lamont yelled. "If I had a candle, I would light it right now. But don't worry. Gordie has a nice little present for you."

Gordie froze! Was Lamont crazy?

"He does? For me? Gordie has a present for *me*?" Lucy ran over. "Thanks, Gordie. Wow! I brought in treats for the class today. But I didn't think anyone would bring *me* a treat."

Lamont smiled. "Well, he did. It will be the one present you will never forget, either."

Lucy smiled. "Boy, I sure got lucky with a locker partner. My own brother forgot it was my birthday!" She walked back into room 9. "Third grade is so nice."

The final bell rang.

Gordie poked Lamont's arm. "Why did you say that?"

"Because you did bring her a present. A stink bomb."

Gordie leaned against the wall. "I can't give it to her now. She's expecting a present. A real present. What if she tells Miss Tingle?"

"She will, too." Lamont nodded. "Girls love to tell the teacher stuff."

"I never planned to get kicked out of the third grade!"

"You better plan something fast," said Lamont. "'Cause here comes Miss Tingle now!"

"I didn't mean it!" cried Gordie. He pressed his back against locker 38.

"What's wrong, Gordie?" asked Miss Tingle. "Are you okay?"

"Are we in trouble?" asked Lamont.

Miss Tingle laughed. "No. I wanted you both to come inside now. It's time for math."

It took Gordie a long time to finish his math page. He stared at his paper. He had to add four dozen apples and two dozen oranges. He couldn't think straight. He kept seeing four stinky sneakers and two hunks of Limburger cheese.

"How many need more time to finish?" asked Miss Tingle.

Gordie raised his hand. Only two other hands went up. Gordie pulled his hand down fast. He didn't want Miss Tingle to think he didn't know how to add fruit.

After Miss Tingle collected the math pages, she said, "I love reading so much. I want all of you to love reading, too. Every day, I will read to you for fifteen minutes."

A few kids clapped. Gordie poked his neck out far to see the book. He hoped it was a chapter book.

"I've decided to read *Charlotte's Web*. This book was written by E. B. White." Miss Tingle held up the book.

Trista covered her eyes. "That book is too sad."

Miss Tingle shook her head. "It's about a very brave pig and a very smart spider. But if it makes us sad, we can stop reading."

"Or skip the sad parts," added Trista. "My dad does that."

Lucy raised her hand. "Miss Tingle, may I pass out my birthday treat? The class can eat it as a snack."

"Good idea, Lucy," said Miss Tingle. "A book and a birthday treat. What a nice idea."

Lucy got out of her seat. She walked to the front of the room and got a big white box. Then she walked down the aisle and let each kid choose a cupcake.

Miss Tingle started to read.

Gordie froze. Did Miss Tingle just say,"Where's Papa going with that ax?" or "Where's Gordie going with that cheese?"

"Go on, pick one," whispered Lucy. She was standing in front of Gordie holding a box of cupcakes with pink and green sprinkles.

Miss Tingle kept on reading. She made her voice sound soft when Fern talked and strong when Pa talked.

Gordie reached out for a cupcake. He set it on his desk.

"Thanks," said Gordie.

"You can take two," Lucy added. "Because you brought me a treat."

Gordie's face went hot. "No, that's okay."

Lucy set the box on Gordie's desk. She reached in and set another cupcake in front of him. "I want you to have two."

Lucy smiled at Gordie. Then she picked up her box and went to the next desk.

Gordie stared at the two cupcakes. Miss Tingle's voice sounded far away. He wanted to listen to the story. But his heart was beating so fast, all he could hear was *thump, thump, thump.*

He had two big problems. Two problems he had never printed in his planner. First of all, he had to think of a birthday present for Lucy. A *nice* present. Then he had to get the stinky cheese out of locker 38.

chapter

When Miss Tingle stopped reading, every-one clapped. Everyone but Gordie. He was too busy staring at the cupcakes.

"Boy, Miss Tingle sure is a good reader," said Lamont. He leaned over and pointed at the cupcakes. "Hey, no fair, Gordie. How come you got two?"

"Because you told Lucy I had a treat for her," snapped Gordie. "A treat I don't have."

Lamont smiled. "Yes you do. The cheese will work. Then I can move into locker 38 with you."

"I can't give her the cheese now."

"Why not?"

"Because . . ." Gordie wasn't sure why he couldn't. He just knew he couldn't. Ruining someone's birthday was worse than mean.

"All right now. Let's take out our spelling books," called Miss Tingle. "After spelling, it's time for gym. I'll let you go to your lockers for your gym shoes."

"Yippee!" cried a few kids. Gym class with Mr. Weber was always fun.

"Oh, no," said Gordie. As soon as Lucy opened the locker, the stink would jump out. The stinky cheese might just roll off the shelf and land on her head.

"What's wrong with you?" asked Lamont. "You look like you just ate some of that stinky cheese."

Gordie's hand shot up. "Miss Tingle!"

"What is it, Gordie?"

"I have to go to the bathroom. I have to go *right now*!"

Lots of kids laughed. Lucy turned around and smiled.

"Go ahead, dear," said Miss Tingle. "But no running in the hall."

Gordie got out of his seat. He walked as fast as he could out the door. He closed the door very quietly. Then he ducked down so Miss Tingle wouldn't see him through the glass. He tiptoed over to locker 38. He put his nose next to the door. He sniffed.

Good! No stinky smell was leaking out. Gordie looked up and down the hall. Then he slowly opened his locker door. He stuck his head all the way inside. It smelled like stinky cheese.

"Oh, no!" whispered Gordie. What if he had ruined Lucy's birthday sweater?

Gordie picked up the pink sleeve of Lucy's sweater. He bent down and gave it a long, long sniff.

"Hey, where's your pass, kid?"

Gordie spun around, nearly bumping into Lumpy Labriola.

"I . . . I needed something in my locker."

Lumpy pushed Gordie aside and grabbed Lucy's sweater. "I bet you look really pretty in this." Lumpy shoved Gordie's face far into the locker, the fuzzy pink sweater smashed against his face.

"Like your new hotel room?" Lumpy asked.

"Gordie, what's going on?" Lucy was standing there, holding a cupcake.

"He's trying on your sweater," Lumpy said.

"Leave him alone," Lucy said. She reached out and grabbed Lumpy's arm. "If you don't let him go right now, I'm telling my oldest brother. You know, the one with the tattoo . . ." She used her bossiest voice.

Gordie felt Lumpy's hands spring off him. He pulled Gordie out of the locker and took the sweater from his face.

"Sorry, Lucy." Lumpy slunk down the hallway.

Gordie hung up Lucy's sweater. "Thanks, Lucy."

Lucy smiled. "Lumpy is okay most of the time. Are you all right?"

"Yeah. But I'm glad you came out here. Where were you going?"

"I wanted to give the principal a cupcake," Lucy said.

"Oh, oh, I see," said Gordie. "Well, I was on my way to the bathroom."

Lucy didn't say anything. She just stood there staring at Gordie.

"But before I go to the bathroom, I wanted to check on our locker," said Gordie.

Lucy smiled. "Is that my surprise?" She pointed to the top shelf.

"Yes—I mean—no," said Gordie. He stared down at the floor. His head felt as heavy as a watermelon. His head was stuffed with tricks, and lies, and . . . and stinky cheese.

Lucy walked to the locker. "Can I have my treat now?"

Gordie didn't know what to do. So he handed Lucy the cheese. "Here. I hope you don't hate it too much."

Lucy had a cupcake in one hand and the cheese in the other hand. "Can you hold the cupcake?"

Gordie took the cupcake. He kept his eyes on the floor. He didn't want to see Lucy start to cry. He didn't want to see Lucy throw the hunk of cheese at his head.

"Oh gosh!" cried Lucy.

Gordie shut his eyes.

"Limburger!" Lucy laughed. "I *love* this cheese."

Gordie's eyes flew open. Lucy was smiling like she was looking at a pretty seashell. Lucy was smelling the cheese like it was a flower.

"You do?" Gordie took a step closer. "My mom thinks it stinks."

"It stinks, but it tastes good. My grannie and I eat this cheese on crackers," said Lucy. "When I go to her house I do two

things. First I walk her dog. Then I go to Mr. DeLuca's store and get Limburger cheese."

Gordie blinked. "Mr. DeLuca? On Elm Street?"

Lucy nodded. "He and Grannie are friends."

Gordie smiled. "He's my grandad."

"Really?" said Lucy. "He's very nice, Gordie. Once Grannie forgot her wallet, and Mr. DeLuca said to just pay him later."

Gordie smiled. His grandad *was* a nice

man. Then he frowned. He stared into the locker, feeling bad. Lucy was nice. She didn't know he wanted to kick her out of their locker.

Lucy wrapped the cheese back in the paper. She put it on the top shelf. "I better give Mr. Fratorolli his cupcake."

Gordie watched Lucy begin to walk down the hall. He looked at the big clock. Soon Miss Tingle would open the door.

"Time for gym," Miss Tingle would say.

Gordie started to close the locker door. The locker was pretty full. One pink sweater, one blue jacket, four gym shoes, and some stinky cheese on the shelf.

Gordie wished he had something nice to give Lucy.

Gordie reached into his pockets, pulling out two rubber bands, a piece of chewing gum with lint on it, and eleven cents. None of it was a good present. He shoved it all into his locker.

"Hey—" Gordie raced down the hall "Hey, Lucy, wait up."

Lucy stopped and turned around.

"Here," said Gordie. He handed her a baseball card. It was the card Lamont had given him yesterday. The player wasn't really famous now. Lucy wouldn't care. She wouldn't even know.

Lucy looked at the card. Gordie bit his lip. Maybe this was a dumb idea. Lucy didn't even know about baseball cards.

"Fastball Martinez," said Lucy. She grinned. "Wow! Thanks, Gordie. I don't have him. He's a decent pitcher. Maybe next year, he will be a *real* good pitcher. My dad gave me a Ken Griffey, Jr., card for my birthday."

"What?" Gordie's mouth fell open. Lucy liked baseball?

"Thanks! What a nice lockermate." Lucy turned and walked down the hall.

Gordie turned around and walked back to room 9. Lucy liked baseball! Wait till he told Lamont. Maybe they could trade cards with her. As soon as he got home, he would get his planner.

Instead of adding: GET LUCY DIAZ OUT OF

LOCKER 38 he would print: BRING SHOE BOX OF CARDS TO TRADE WITH LAMONT AND LUCY.

Maybe he and Lucy could pick a few cards to tape to the locker.

Miss Tingle opened the door, and the class came out into the hall to line up for gym.

"Where have you been?" Lamont asked Gordie. "I thought Lucy stuffed you into the locker."

"No. I gave her the cheese. She wasn't mad. She liked it."

Lamont shook his head. "That girl is nuts! How are you going to get her out of your locker? Do you have a new plan?"

Gordie grinned. "Yeah. I'm planning to let her stay in the locker."

"But, all summer we planned to share a locker with each other," said Lamont. "It's on page three of your planner, Gordie."

"I know. But we can try to share a locker next year. And in fifth grade, too."

Lamont laughed. "Maybe we can share a locker in college."

Gordie and Lamont slapped each other a high five to seal their plan. Gordie turned around and closed locker 38. Once it was decorated, it would be the best locker in the school. And since even Lumpy Labriola was afraid of Lucy, locker 38 didn't need a lock. All it needed was more baseball cards.

Gordie hurried over and got in line. Third grade was a lot of fun.

He couldn't have planned it any better.